GOLDEN

GOLD HOCKEY #19.5

ELISE FABER

GOLD HOCKEY SERIES

Changed
Scored

GOLDEN
BY ELISE FABER
Newsletter sign-up

GOLDEN

Copyright © 2024 Elise Faber
Ebook ISBN-13: 978-1-63749-135-5

ONE

Pascal

I SHOULDN'T BE HERE.

Shouldn't be watching her from the shadows, watching her through her bedroom window.

It's disgusting—me being a fucking Peeping Tom, not the beautiful woman curled up in her pajamas, her son beside her as the two of them watch *Great British Bake Off* on the big screen TV mounted on the far wall.

But I *am* here.

Soaking in every single moment of her, of this glimpse into her life.

Lauren pastes a smile on her face, pretends to be perfectly happy when she's in the outside world, always putting on a brave face for her son, but I've watched her holding him as he cries. I've seen the tears streak down her own cheeks. I've even heard her tell him it's okay to cry, to miss his dad.

Who fought for them but died anyway.

Fucking cancer.

But though she's given that slice of vulnerability mixed with strength to her son—something that's a fuckton better than any of the buck-up-and-move-on parenting advice good old Mom and Dad gave me, the rest of the world only gets an impenetrable wall.

Or maybe that's just me.

Because she's close to Lucas, the fucker.

She talks to him.

And Sara. And Blane. And most of the other fuckers on the Gold hockey team.

Me, on the other hand?

Brick. *Fucking*. Wall.

Sighing, I tuck the binoculars away—a set that I can't technically get legally on the free market, but a pair that I have access to because I have *connections*. *Connections* that I don't want to have, *connections* that I've tried to distance myself from, but also *connections* that allow me and my company of specialized security to get our hands on equipment that makes our job safer and easier.

Equipment that allows me to play Peeping Tom.

On a woman who's so fucking beautiful it takes my breath away, and her son, who has been through more than he should at his young age but has the same core of brightness his mother possesses.

Drawing me in like a moth to the golden flame.

"It's only because she's alone," I mutter, turning away from the house, finding it harder than it should be to slip into the shadows. But I manage to pull back, cutting across a couple of back yards, winding my way to my car that's parked several blocks over. "Her being alone is the only reason I do this."

A lie.

But it's a lie I have to tell myself, otherwise I'll look too closely, think too much, be too...

"Shut the fuck up," I grumble under my breath, yanking myself out of my head as I check behind me, searching for tails. It's standard operating procedure for me—the checks, the extra measures of safety. It's why my profession is security, is putting myself on the line to protect good people.

People who are untouched by those connections I hold.

I slip out, confident that—as usual—no one has seen me.

I'm fucking good at my job.

I have to be.

Otherwise people get dead.

So, when I unlock my car, the soft bleep pairing with the lights flashing, and I see something tucked under one of the wiper blades, my gut clenches.

It could be an advertisement, one of those bullshit fliers some asshole likes to paper every car in the neighborhood with.

But I *know* it's not.

All my precautions, my safety measures—living carefully, constantly looking over my shoulder...none of that fucking matters.

Because of those goddamned *connections*.

"Fuck," I mutter, moving forward, my boots clipping on the pavement now that I'm not bothering to be fucking sneaky. I yank the folded paper out, get one glimpse of the handwriting and I know.

Fucking *know*.

That a barrage of shit is about to rain down on my life.

I look around, searching the darkness surrounding me on all sides, searching for the one person who's always been able to hide from me, who's always been able to track me down, no matter how hard I fought to remain in the shadows.

But, like always, I don't find him.

I just...know he's there.

Crumpling the paper, I make a show of tossing it into the passenger's seat, like I don't give a fuck what's inside. But my heart is pounding as I sit in the driver's seat, start up the engine and drive away. My body is tense as I take the long way back to headquarters, using my alternate routes, zigzagging through city streets, before finally slipping into a nondescript warehouse that serves as my team's command center and the only home I've ever had—because I cobbled it together, secured the fragile, ugly pieces together with duct tape and twine.

The reinforced metal panel rolls closed with a *clang* behind my car and I get out, punch in my code at the first door, making sure it locks behind me before I start winding through the hallways. I have to punch in two more codes, the last one paired with a retinal scan, before I make it fully inside and walk by the rows of desks, each loaded with top-of-the-line equipment. But at this time of night, those desks are empty, and the screens are all off—none of our clients are currently requiring twenty-four-hour video monitoring.

So, my guys are either traveling one-on-one with our clientele, providing security for various actors and athletes and professional sports teams, or—in rare cases—are taking some much-needed time off.

Even though I'm the only one here, I still don't unfold the note, don't read the words written in a hand I know better than my own—not until I'm inside my office with the door closed.

The paper crinkles as I flatten it out.

My heart sinks as my eyes move across the page, as I see what's written there.

Because it confirms all the fears that knotted my fucking insides the moment I saw the note tucked underneath the wiper blade.

And now—because of me—Lauren is in danger.

TWO

Lauren

"CAN WE, MOM?" Matteo begs, his big brown eyes pleading as he looks up at me. "Can we?"

I turn my gaze from my son, my heart, the boy I live for, and meet the eyes of a slender blonde with sad chocolate-colored eyes.

Brit Plantain, star goalie of the Gold, has been through a lot over the last year—in retirement, out of retirement, finding her place back on the roster, and then facing a major injury that almost ended her career (though she's in the lineup for the upcoming season as the backup goalie, bringing experience and strength in the locker room—and much-needed prowess between the pipes), and she was also there for the shooting.

A deranged drug dealer firing on a group of people, on a collective of the Gold, who had gotten together to enjoy each other's company and some ice cream on a beautiful warm evening.

Trying to hurt us in the worst possible way.

Because...he targeted Vivi, an innocent teenager with a spine of steel who had survived...too freaking much.

And Matteo.

There had been a gun pointed in his direction, my brave little boy who tried to put himself between Vivi and that gunman.

Shots had been fired, but somehow, neither Vivi nor Matteo were injured.

Instead, it was a player on the Gold, Lucas, who had ended up with two bullet wounds that had nearly taken his life.

He's okay now, all of these months later, his return to the ice slated to happen soon, but the nightmares linger.

For all of us.

I almost witnessed the life being extinguished from my baby's eyes.

So, just managing to park on this street is a feat. Getting out, standing on this sidewalk, and staring out at the swooping lines of twinkling lights has my heart in my throat. Because beyond those beautifully draped glowing bulbs and the thick trunks of one-hundred-year-old oak trees, is a large, grassy field.

And on that field...

I almost lost Matteo.

A shudder rakes down my spine.

"Please?" he says, grabbing my hand and bouncing up and down.

I shake off the fear, force a smile at my baby who's not really a baby anymore, but rather a big boy—his words, not mine—and say, "Of course we can, honey."

He whoops and takes off running, and I have to clench my

teeth together in order to not call him back, to not chase after him, to not bundle him up in my car and drive away. To run. To hide. To never *ever* risk him.

But...he can't live like that. It's not healthy, not good for him emotionally, socially, and—

Frankly, it's not good for me either.

I can't keep hiding from my life, making every single bit of my future about him.

Next up, he and I will be on that reality show *sMothered*.

Which is why I don't call him back to me, don't stop him from joining the influx of Gold kids running around like maniacs on the grass on this warm fall evening, don't pull him away from this family of hearts and team and sport rather than blood. I don't stop him even though I want to.

Because he needs to live.

And if he's okay being here, I'll be here too.

"You don't have to do this alone, you get that, right?" Brit's face has gentled, and I know she sees right through me, right through the wall I slapped up around my emotions, sees that I'm forcing myself forward and it's fucking hard. But—

"You have room to talk," I tell her. Gently. Because she's had a rough year and hasn't exactly come to me for help.

Two peas in a pod we are.

A flash of emotions across her face—guilt, worry, and finally chagrin. "Yeah, well," she mutters. "Apparently, it takes one to know one."

I reach out and take her hand, feeling the callouses on her palm, her fingers, knowing they've been born from years and years of hard work. I never had callouses like that, not until we lost Dave.

I was a freaking princess.

No mowing lawns or taking out trash. Not even filling my

car up with gas. And it wasn't like I was stuck with all of the housework, either. My job was Matteo—taking care of our baby when Dave wasn't home.

Because when he was, it was father-son time.

And I could take a bath, go for a walk, sleep, or watch my trash TV.

Dave just...filled every space of my life—so much so that I wasn't sure who I was until he was gone.

I had to pay bills and do all of the cooking, all of the cleaning. The yard work. The grocery shopping and meal planning and making sure our cars—no, *my* car because I sold his and put the money in Matteo's college fund—was in regularly for service. Registering for school, buying hockey equipment, making sure Matteo had playdates and his homework done and—

All of it.

By myself.

It was awful.

But I learned something important, something big since he's been gone, since I went from being protected and put onto a shelf to having to navigate through scary channels and grinding out a life.

I learned that I *can* do it all by myself. That I don't need to be taken care of. It's nice. It was fucking wonderful to have all that care while I had it, but it's not my future.

I can't be in another relationship like that. I'll shrink. I'll lose myself. My existence will be my boys, and only my boys.

I love Matteo. I loved Dave.

So fucking much.

I just...need more.

"Okay then," I say, knowing Brit's lingering here on the sidewalk, here in the shadows because she's worried about me.

Because she cares about everyone else, sometimes to the detriment of herself.

I squeeze her hand, start drawing her forward.

"Let's do it together."

THREE

Pascal

"WHY IS it that the Gold like their ice cream so fucking much?" Delaney mutters from next to me.

Our company isn't strictly on hire for nights like these—not now that the dealer is behind bars for the rest of his life and the risk of any of the other threats have been investigated, dismissed, or eliminated—but when I hear from my sources that the Gold are going for ice cream—a-fucking-gain—I make sure I'm here.

Because I almost wasn't here in time before.

Because Matteo and Vivi and Logan—

Well, I just make sure I'm fucking here, okay?

Tonight, one of my agents, Delaney, is with me, trailing along even though I offered to drop her at the complex.

"What else do I have to do?" she said when I offered, and...well, that's a feeling I understand.

What else do I have to do except lurk in the shadows and watch people live their lives?

It used to be that satisfied the itch in me—watching

people have happiness, rooting for them to get through their shit, helping where I could, shifting a few pieces, ensuring they ran into each other, protecting the people they loved.

But, eventually, I started to buy into the bullshit that is this hockey team.

I started to believe that maybe enough time had passed and I could...

"It's bullshit."

The words coming out of my mouth, instead of staying in my head—where they fucking belong—display a dangerous breach of control.

Luckily, Delaney doesn't pick up on that.

Probably because her eyes are locked on the field.

Locked on a certain hockey player.

"It *is* bullshit," she mutters. "The empty calories alone in that soft serve. They're supposed to be professional athletes. Don't they have a meal plan to follow?"

"Cheat Days," I say, like that's an explanation.

And I suppose it is. Their dietician is a control freak who likes to plan things out months in advance—including Cheat Days that align so the guys and their families can get together like this.

The off-season is different, with the team scattering to their home countries or to the East Coast or Midwest to visit families, but a lot of the old-timers have long-term contracts that mean they've put down firm roots here in the Bay Area for the remainder of the year.

Their kids are in local schools, have friends who were born and raised here. Lives that are built around this area.

Thus, California has its hooks into them for ten months out of the year, and travel home is restricted to the small window after the playoffs and before training camp.

But the meal plan allows for that.

Because...planning.

And Rebecca's life is finding more efficient and healthy ways to fuel their bodies, so the off-season is sorted too.

Right along with nights at The Dairy.

"Ridiculous," Delaney mutters.

I disagree with her, but I don't say it out loud. Mostly because I used to be where she was.

Fresh out of the shit, searching for some peace, not understanding how in the fuck these people could possibly trust each other. A big family. Lots of personalities. Hardly any biology between them—though, God knows, biology doesn't mean shit.

Still, these people have it figured out.

And that's why I'm here.

Because that's a beautiful thing—I get that now—and it deserves to be protected.

"Have you ever eaten the ice cream here?" I ask, seeing a little boy run across the grass—

No. Not a little boy. Seeing *Matteo* running across the grass. I tense, gaze searching, muscles going taut, remembering what happened the last time we were all here on a warm fall evening.

Remembering how I failed.

And how I'm going to make sure I don't, not fucking ever again.

Things need to fucking change.

I can't keep playing by the same fucked-up rules I erected around my life.

I need to do something different.

Which is why I ignore Delaney gaping at me as I step out of the shadows.

"The mint chocolate chip is pretty fucking good," I tell

her as I turn toward the slender brunette—Lauren—who's walking next to a tall blond—Brit.

I might have fucked up my life over and over again, have disappointed the people who meant more to me than anything else, failed them time and again, failed them so intensely that I don't deserve what so many people on this field have found. I don't deserve happiness or another chance at love, or to even be a peripheral part of this family.

But Delaney does.

She deserves more. She deserves *everything*.

And so does Lauren.

And Brit.

Which is why I'm making the choice to not fuck around. I'm going to draw out the threat, flush the bastard who's haunted my life from the shadows.

And I'm going to make these women's lives better.

Then I'll slip away, will disappear back to where I belong.

The lonely darkness.

"Come on," I toss over my shoulder toward my newest agent, causing Delaney's mouth to fall open even more. "I'll buy you a cone."

FOUR

Lauren

"THAT'LL BE EIGHT-FIFTY," the teenager in the ball cap with The Dairy branded T-shirt says.

They recently upgraded their equipment from an ancient cash register to sleek new tablets which means instead of the whirring and clacking of the keys, I hear faint tapping that reminds me of Matteo battling Creepers on his tablet.

I shudder but double-tap the side button on my phone, pulling up my mobile payment card, start to extend it toward the reader he holds out.

But I don't get close enough to tap.

Or the magical distance that makes the payment connect.

Because warm fingers wrap around my wrist, pulling my phone back, a softly accented voice hitting my ears. "Can you add two mint chocolate chip cups to that?"

I blink, mouth falling open at Pascal, who's appeared like he always does—out of nowhere. "Do you even eat ice cream?" I ask, gaze sliding down that hard, muscled body and then back up.

Unfathomable dark brown eyes hold mine for a moment, not long enough for me to read the emotions in them. Not that I would even be able to—what with that wall he's erected between himself and the rest of the world. It's thick and impenetrable.

If I hadn't seen him display a sly sense of humor with Brit and a few of the others, I would have thought this man is a robot.

Of course, he was very *un*-robot like when Matteo was face-to-face with a gun—

Enough.

He lifts his hand so quick that I almost flinch back, but it doesn't make contact with my face. He halts it an inch away from my skin, the tip of his fingers so near my cheek that I can feel the heat of him.

I could lean in.

Could feel the brush of them over my flesh.

But even as I think that, he drops his hand back to his side, says, "Of course, I eat ice cream."

My brows lift as my gaze drifts down, taking in all six-foot-plus of his big, muscular frame. He doesn't have an ounce of fat on his body.

Those abs of his...

A fucking miracle for the female populace.

So him eating ice cream?

Doesn't fit.

But here he is...ordering ice cream.

"Um," the teenager with the tablet says, "so two mint chocolate chips, a strawberry shortcake, and a peanut butter swirl. Is there anything else I can get you guys?"

Pascal glances down at me. "For you and Matteo?"

I nibble at my bottom lip, feeling my heart skip a beat

when there's a flare of...something behind those dark brown eyes. "Yeah," I whisper after a moment.

"Did Brit order anything?"

My heart skips another beat because Brit had turned toward the line with me, talking about a banana brownie sundae, but then had been waylaid by the kids.

Smiling softly, I nod toward the grass where the kids are holding a makeshift soccer game. "She got conned into joining Matteo and Vivi and the others."

He studies me for another long moment, seeming to stare straight into my mind, to pluck thoughts—inappropriate ones about how my body reacts when he's near—from my mind.

Or maybe, he's just like how everyone says: hyper-observant and vigilant and way too smart for his own good.

Either way, his gaze points back toward the teenager, and he says softly, "And can you please add a banana brownie sundae with extra cherries, nuts, and whipped cream."

A hand reaches into my chest and squeezes tightly around my heart.

He knows Brit's order.

Of course he does.

I inhale, throat tight.

Wanting to know more about this man. Wanting to understand what makes him tick.

Like always.

"Sure thing, man," the teenager says. "That'll be twenty-two dollars."

I start to extend my phone a second time, but warm fingers are wrapping around my wrist again, the slightly roughened fingertips brushing gently over my skin, making me shiver as Pascal passes over some cash. "Keep the change."

Wide teenage eyes—probably because that was far more

than twenty-two dollars. "Thanks, man. I'll have those right out for you."

Pascal nods and then he's resting a palm on my back, turning us away from the front of the line, shepherding us toward the waiting area. We've barely slid to a halt before his hand drops and he's shifting, tugging off his jacket, settling it around my shoulders.

"Oh," I say, trying to tug it off, intending to pass it back over. "I'm not—"

He grasps the lapels, holds them together, and crouches slightly so that our gazes align, holding my stare just long enough for me to read in his that I'm not going to win this battle.

And...part of me doesn't want to.

The coat is warm and smells like spice and male and Pascal and it's been such a long time since I've had a man's scent in my nose that I find myself inhaling, trying to sear the fragrance into my lungs.

Because who knows when I'll have something like this again.

Because Dave is gone.

Because my life is Matteo now—and it will always be.

"Do you—" he begins, but then his eyes slant over my shoulder and I find myself turning, following that look, seeing a beautiful woman with sleek black hair, a confident stride, and a body that can kill—literally, it looks like she could kill a bad guy with her pinky finger—come our way. "Do you know Delaney?" he asks, and I tear my gaze from that gorgeous female and look back up at Pascal.

I shake my head.

"Lauren. Delaney," he says when she's close enough to hear. "Delaney. Lauren."

She smiles at me, and it's as beautiful as she is. "Nice to meet you," she says, sticking out her hand for me to shake.

Which I do.

And then she's releasing my hand, moving to Pascal's side, leaning close, her lips going to his ear.

Something slices through my heart, deep and leaving me with a huge wound that I have no business possessing. Because my brain is putting the rest of the pieces together.

Pascal and Delaney.

Tall and strong and confident.

Gorgeous and beautiful.

"Two mint chocolate chip cups?"

I turn and see the teenager approaching, watch as he passes Pascal the two cups before returning to the kitchen for the rest of our order.

"Here," Pascal says, passing it over to her.

The woman smiles, lashes dancing on the tops of her cheek. "Thanks, *honey*."

Honey.

It doesn't sit quite right, like the tone is off, or maybe the endearment doesn't make sense sliding off her lips.

But before I can really suss that out, I hear, "Mom!" and turn in time to see Matteo barreling toward me. "I scored a goal!" he all but shouts, drawing a smile from Pascal and Delaney and a high five from me.

"Nice, bud," I say. "And I think that's perfect timing because—"

"A peanut butter swirl?" the teenager, with full hands, announces.

"Yes!" Matteo says with a fist bump, taking the treat and running off, making me hold my breath and send a prayer up to the universe that he—and the ice cream—don't take a tumble before I turn back and accept the other desserts.

I'm juggling my spoon and Brit's banana brownie sundae as my gaze slides to the side again.

I see Pascal and Delaney standing close.

And I think...they fit.

Of course his girlfriend is a woman like her.

FIVE

Pascal

DELANEY HAS BEEN DRAWN into the game—exactly as I knew she would be—and is now running with the kids, kicking the soccer ball around, her hair slipping from her ponytail, spreading out over her shoulders and flying behind her like a sleek, black cape.

It's a beautiful sight—anyone could objectively see that.

But it's not why I'm watching her.

Nope...it's the way a certain hockey player is watching her.

Eyes glued, gaze tracking in a way that I know means...it won't be long before her future is further entwined with these people.

Good.

Mission accomplished.

"Your girlfriend is beautiful."

I turn my head toward Lauren, but not in surprise. I felt her approaching, felt her presence coming close, and not just because of my training, but because my body is so in tune with hers that I can feel her take a breath within a hundred-yard vicinity.

Hyperbole.

But...I knew she was there.

Her words, though, don't make one bit of fucking sense.

"Who?" I ask, tilting my head to the side, studying her closely—and then *more* closely—when her cheeks go pink.

"Um." She nibbles at her bottom lip. "Your girlfriend." She clears her throat. "She's beautiful."

I frown, because I'm smart, but I don't know what in the fuck all Lauren is talking about. "I don't have a girlfriend, sweets."

"Oh." A beat, teeth worrying her bottom lip. "Your date then?"

My brows draw together.

Now a dash of impatience creeps into her eyes and she jerks her chin toward the game in progress. "The woman you *came* with?"

Clarity hits me like a two-by-four to the temple and I know I'm a dumbass. I can disassemble an M24 rifle, clean it, and put the pieces back together in under ten minutes, but I'm not good at understanding women.

Or women like Lauren, anyway.

Women with a golden soul and a beautiful heart and—

I've lost my fucking mind.

I'm standing out of the shadows, having eaten ice cream—that's now sitting like lead in my stomach—because I'm trying to draw out my past, eliminate it, and disappear back *into* the shadows. I can't be talking about beautiful hearts and golden souls and—

I need to focus.

"Delaney works for me at the security company," I tell her

before turning back to the scene in front of us. "And she has a crush on a hockey player."

"Um."

I look back.

Lauren's brows are forming twin rainbows that are arched halfway up her forehead. "Which hockey player?" she asks, gaze swinging away, head tilting.

Studying the group for several beats.

Then she glances back at me.

I shake my head. "I don't divulge secrets."

Her expression turns incredulous. "You just told me that she has a crush on a hockey player!"

"But you don't know which hockey player," I point out.

Am I grasping at straws because she's right? Yes, I fucking am.

Luckily, she scowls, looking back out at the field again for a long moment before shaking her head. She glances up at me, nose wrinkling. "You're right. With all of these new guys on the team, it could be anyone."

Winning Stanley Cups. Retirement. Salary caps and injuries and trades. All of that means...rebuilding.

Fresh blood.

Young guys.

Young *single* guys.

Of which Delaney likes one.

My lips twitch and Lauren gives a disgruntled sigh that has them twitching further.

Because I haven't seen her annoyed—and I've watched her a lot.

Which means that this side of her has alarm bells blaring in my mind.

Because instead of making me less interested, less capti-vated, less fucking obsessed, I want to know more. What else irritates her? What else has her blowing out that tiny stream of hot air I can feel on the side of my neck?

What else don't I know about her?

It doesn't matter.

Get her safe. Find her a man to look after her, worship her, to complete hers and Matteo's life.

No matter that it makes that ice cream in my stomach turn to concrete.

No matter that it makes me want to commit murder—and *I'm* the one planning on orchestrating this shit.

"Right," Lauren says after a long moment, awkward quiet having fallen between us. "Well, I'd better get back to—"

"How was Matteo's spelling test?" I blurt out, some part of me needing to keep her close.

A fucking idiotic part.

But...that part has spoken out loud.

Lauren freezes, looks up at me with wide eyes.

And I realize my idiocy knows no bounds.

Because how the fuck would I know about the spelling test?

Well, genius, I only know about it because I watched them study for it through the windows of her house.

But I can't exactly tell her that now, can I?

Sure can't.

Thankfully, I'm trained at removing myself from potentially volatile situations.

And I remember that, this year, her son is in the same class as Sara's. Sara is a former gold-medal-winning figure skater and client who needed my services for a short time. Her husband used to play for the Gold, and even though Mike was a dick of epic proportions at one point, he'd turned out all right.

They are both here tonight.

I nod toward them. "Mike mentioned it," I lie.

Her head tilts again as she studies me. "Oh," she murmurs. "Right. Well, he got a hundred percent."

Pride settles somewhere deep. "Of course he did." Then I say, fucking stupidly, "Because he has a mom who helped him study."

Information I couldn't know without being a Peeping Tom—or couldn't know for sure, anyway—but, thankfully, she doesn't pick up on that.

Likely because we have a gaggle of children heading our way.

Led by a secret agent with payback in her eyes.

Or maybe murder.

Either way, I hear Matteo even amongst that gaggle of excited—and loud—voices that surround us in an instant. "Pascal!" he shouts. "You're on my team!"

And then he takes my hand, drawing me forward, Vivi trailing us in that careful way she's done since I put myself between her and the gun. I know she sticks close because she feels safe, but her nearness reminds me of my failure to look after the people I was supposed to protect.

Now *and* then.

The past sweeps up, threatens to yank me back under.

I want to sprint for the shadows, slip back into watching instead of being drawn along with this family.

This is dangerous and stupid, and I have that past to track down.

But...I had to have ice cream.

And now, apparently, I'm playing soccer, unable to tell a kid who's been through too much no.

Fucking pathetic.

And I know the man watching me from those shadows will think so too.

SIX

Lauren

"BEN INVITED me to sleep over at his house," Matteo says a couple of hours later, grabbing my hand and tugging lightly, drawing my stare away from where Pascal is talking to Delaney.

Who's *not* his girlfriend.

Which makes me feel...

Something that I'm not ready for, something that's scary and intense and...just scary.

I inhale softly, shove the thoughts out of my head.

My life is Matteo.

My life is Matteo.

Be happy, baby girl. Live a big, beautiful life for our son.

Dave's voice in my mind has my eyes stinging, throat clogging.

God, I miss him.

The man he was and all that we weren't able to create together.

And all that he missed out on, all that Matteo and I lost too.

It's been three years since we lost Dave, but truthfully, he was lost to Matteo and me before that. Fucking cancer. It kills the joy in people's lives, sucks the fun from lighthearted moments, shadows the happy memories, clings to everything that was remotely pleasant like flesh-eating bacteria, slowly eroding any contentment.

Now, after that long battle Dave fought and I did my best to help him through, I often struggle to remember my husband on our wedding day, on our honeymoon, when he held my hand in the delivery room as I brought Matteo into this world. Instead I remember a different hospital room. A different man. A different body. A different lifetime.

And sometimes, I wonder what Matteo remembers.

Does he have any of the joy of hikes and piggyback rides?

Or does he just remember the exhaustion pulling at Dave's limbs, the pain he tried to hide, the sadness burned into our home—

"Mom?"

I grind my teeth together, blink the past away. "Yeah, honey?"

"Ben invited me to sleep over at his house tonight." He bounces on his toes, body wiggling in excitement. "Can I, Mom? Can I please? It's not a school night and his parents say it's okay and Alex and Roxie are coming too."

"Let me look at the calendar, baby," I say, pulling out my phone, mostly trying to delay.

He's never been to a sleepover.

What if he gets scared?

What will I do without him at home?

Alone. With my thoughts.

I shudder.

Matteo opens his mouth and I know he's going to ask me again—in that sweet, pleading voice that never fails to melt my heart.

I know it'll be near on impossible for me to resist him.

I *can* say no.

I'm a mom—saying no can be my superpower.

It's just...I like it when I can tell him yes.

He's had too many noes already.

No, we can't go to the park, Daddy isn't feeling well. No, we can't play music or watch that show, Daddy is sleeping. No, we can't go to that birthday party, I have to work and there's no one to pick you up from daycare and take you. No, you can't play hockey right now, we need to take care of Dad (and it's too expensive with the crippling medical debt because our freaking country has made healthcare a business instead of a right).

And too many more.

So, I want to say yes.

I also can't—however—with good conscience, subject another parent to the torture of a sleepover without doing them the courtesy of at least checking with them first.

"The calendar is clear," I say and then add quickly before he can continue with the pleading, "I need to talk to Sara and Mike, honey," I rub a hand over the shorn locks that are the result of his most-recent haircut (bye-bye curls and hello clean-cut military that reminds me of a certain sexy security chief I want to lick all over).

I freeze, heart suddenly in my throat.

Because that's not something I've felt—

Well, that's not my life now.

Matteo scowls, luckily, pulling me from my panic, and I settle my hand on his shoulder, squeeze lightly. "And anyway," I say, "if they *do* say yes, we'll have to go home and pack your bag first, right?" He nods. "So, I need to get all the deets."

He sighs, shaking his head like the way too mature seven-year-old he's become. "No one says deets anymore, Mom."

"Well, I do," I tell him then nudge him forward. "I see some trash on the ground over there. Can you go throw that away and make sure we've left the field clean? I'll talk to Ben's mom and dad." Another nod, this one filled with excited puppy-esque energy (probably because Ben's parents—Sara and Mike—are heading my way, and he's likely to get a positive response to his sleepover request in the next few minutes). Then he's off, sprinting toward the stray napkin that's blowing across the grass.

I watch him scoop it up, run it to the garbage can, then turn toward another piece of trash.

Not doing the bare minimum.

Nope, my kid cares and excels and always goes the extra mile.

God, I love him.

"You've raised a great kid," Mike says, coming to stand next to me.

"The best," I murmur, forcing my eyes away from my heart that's running around outside my body and turning to face him and Sara, who are looking on as Ben and Roxie and the others join in and I know the field is going to be clean in no time. "But that's just him. *He's* the best."

Sara nudges my shoulder with hers. "And maybe he has a great mom."

This.

This right here.

This is why I found myself pulled into the Gold family. Because they're fucking nice. Because they're the hype men (and women) who are supposed to be what family is.

Not tearing down. Not shitting on each other.

Just...respect and love and the supportive backbone when mine threatens to fail.

Not that there isn't shit-giving.

That's hockey.

But it's not mean, and it doesn't hurt, and—

God, my eyes are stinging again.

I blow out a silent breath, nudge Sara's shoulder back, letting her know I hear her and I appreciate the sentiment, and then I focus on the present and the current crisis in front of me.

Because that's all I can do.

One step forward at a time.

"So," I say, "I hear my son is trying to get himself an invite to your house."

Mike chuckles, shakes his head.

Sara grins. "I think my kids were the ringleaders," she admits. "Because between Ben and his sisters, half the team's kids are spending the night at our house." A roll of her eyes. "All of which to say, Matteo is more than welcome to stay, so long as you're okay with it."

My heart squeezes. "That sounds like...a lot."

"Well," Sara says with a shrug. "I figure if we're going to be tortured with a sleepover, we might as well get it over all at once, rather than experience the torment of giggling girls and loudly played video games and hours and hours of hide and seek over three separate weekends."

Maybe I shouldn't let Matteo go.

Because I would have to reciprocate, right?

And that sounds like...

Torture.

But even as I think that, I'm already saying, "If you're sure, then I know that he'd love to join in—"

"Yes!"

All three of our heads whip to the side, see that Matteo, Ben, Alex, and Roxie are standing there with huge grins on their faces.

"Sleepover!" they yell, running off.

"Right," Mike mutters to Sara. "I think we'll just let them run that off for a while. Maybe then we'll actually get some sleep tonight."

"Good idea," she says, lifting her fist for him to bump before glancing back at me. "Do you want to head out and enjoy your free night while we let them tire themselves out? We can swing by your place on the way home and get his stuff."

No, I don't want to leave my baby here without me.

But...I also don't have a reason to stay.

I gird my loins, thank them in advance, and make sure they have my number and address correct, and then I corral my kiddo into a hug and a quiet moment to let him know he can call me, no matter the hour, and to clean up after himself and treat Mr. and Mrs. Stewart with respect, and to be nice to his friends and—

He sighs. "I'll be on my best behavior, Mom."

"Of course you will," I murmur, allowing myself one more hug before I step back, wave to Sara and Mike and Brit, who's joined them, apparently in no hurry to continue on with her evening either.

But I manage to tear myself away from my son, manage to walk my ass to my car, manage to turn on the ignition and drive home.

Where I busy myself packing him everything he might possibly need—and likely far too much—for his first sleepover.

He shows up just as I'm tucking his toothbrush into his backpack and he's so excited and in such a hurry to get back into the SUV with his friends that I barely get more than a drive-by hug and a, "Bye, Mom!" before he's tearing off down the driveway, clambering back into the SUV, and slamming the door shut behind him.

God.

My eyes, they burn.

But I manage to hold it together as I wave to Sara and Mike, as I watch the SUV pull out of the driveway.

As my baby disappears out of sight.

I slam the door behind me, wrench the lock closed, and sink to the floor.

Then I give into those tears.

A LONG WHILE LATER—AND after a long cry because my baby is growing up and I can't stop time—I've gotten it back together.

And...maybe I'm sort of enjoying myself.

The quiet and being able to watch whatever trash I want to watch without having to constantly listen for Matteo coming down the hall and having to pause the TV (because, heaven forbid, he see any of the show I'm consuming). Being able to lounge in the bath without him knocking on the door and asking if we can play basketball.

Because—of course—I'm going to play basketball. Always. Any freaking time.

Take that opportunity. Hold those moments close.

You never know when they'll be gone.

But when he's off having the time of his life—and I know that thanks to Sara texting me pictures of the madness (and a Silly String) battle—I can take a little bit of time to enjoy the first "Me Time" I've had since...

Well, since Dave got sick.

I exhale and toss the remote to the side, glancing at the picture of the three of us I keep on the nightstand, and feel that familiar pang.

It's just...not as sharp as it used to be.

I'll always miss my late husband, but so much has changed since we lost him.

I'm different, and capable of more than I ever thought.

And...I'm okay.

Really, *really* okay.

Maybe that's why, for the first time since that picture was taken, I find myself lifting the frame from the distressed wood of my nightstand and carrying it close to my chest as I pad through the living room and set it on the shelf.

With my other memories.

With the past.

I exhale, intending to turn back for the bedroom, intending to text Sara, letting her know—again—that I'll come, no matter the hour, and head off to sleep.

And that's when there's a heavy knock on my front door.

I jump, knocking the frame over, heart in my throat.

"Ignore it," I whisper.

But some part of me can't.

So, I walk over, peer through the window, and—

My heart catches.

SEVEN

Pascal

I SAT in the shadows and watched her cry.

Like a lump of fucking useless man.

I sat in the shadows while she suffered alone and did nothing.

Just like—

I clench my teeth together so tightly that a sharp bolt of pain slices through my jaw.

But it's enough to center me, to shove those memories deep down, to lock them away, forget they exist.

I can't think about her now.

I can't *remember* now.

Because I'm standing in the shadows, watching Lauren again, seeing the toll it's taking on her to let her son be a normal kid, doing normal things, and my respect is growing for her by the second.

And my obsession.

Which had already grown to fucking troublesome proportions before tonight.

Now…it's closing in on me from all sides, sending me sliding toward the edge of a cliff that's crumbling beneath my feet.

I'm already on my belly, limbs sprawled in all directions, trying to disperse my weight so I don't go plummeting toward the canyon below. I know it's not going to be enough. The edge is breaking apart beneath me.

And I still can't fucking stop watching her.

Especially now that she's emerged from the bathroom, her skin dewy and pink, her hair piled on top of her head, her robe tied around her body—

I freeze, don't tear my gaze from the window, from the woman inside who's so fucking beautiful it takes my breath away, but I'm not seeing *her* any longer. Every single one of my senses is focused behind me.

On the man who's creeping closer, trying to—

I whip around, grab his wrist, and yank him toward me, snapping the bones with one sharp move that has his hand spasming open, dropping the gun. I kick it away—

And then it's…messy.

Fists meeting flesh, air pushed from lungs, grunts escaping. Nails digging, feet kicking, bodies battling.

He's good. And strong.

But I'm better. And stronger.

I get him pinned, his face in the dirt, hands restrained behind his back, my knee digging into his spine as I reach into his back pocket and yank out his cell phone, swiping up and shifting his body enough to get his face to unlock the screen.

Then I'm hitting the contact of the man behind this bullshit.

"Pascal," he says lightly, picking up the call after the first ring.

"Felix."

A beat. "Is he still breathing?"

"Is that concern I detect?" I say softly, listening and restraining, but also hyper-aware of my surroundings.

Because I wouldn't put it past him to stab me in the fucking back.

He's done it before.

Felix's soft laugh tells me that nothing's changed in the ten years since I got out. "Only for my own time. That one took a long fucking time to train. I'm too busy as it is."

I pull in a breath through my nostrils. "But not too busy to be here."

Another laugh. "You know why I'm making my presence known now."

Yeah, I do.

Because he wants my help.

"I'm out of this shit," I remind him. "And I've been out for a decade."

He laughs quietly. "You're never completely out."

There's some truth to that, but that's also why—after I fucking lost everything—I made sure to cover my ass...

And to have plenty of blackmail material.

"I'm out," I say again. "Use someone else."

More laughter. "*Pascal.*"

And I know I'm about to burn some of that blackmail material.

Not the biggest.

But what will hit Felix the hardest.

"New Hampshire," I say softly.

There's no laughter now, no response for a long, long moment. "That's not a pin you can pull."

The fucker below me bucks and I dig my knee harder into his back. "Try me."

To him.

To Felix.

Another long moment of quiet. "This woman is worth that?"

"This woman is innocent," I say. "She and her son stay out of our shit. Permanently."

More quiet. I know he's thinking, he's calculating every angle, trying to figure out which brick to pull without sending the entire archway down on his head.

The trouble—for him—is that if I let out what he did in New Hampshire...

He'll be fucked.

Criminally *and* financially.

Felix clicks his tongue. "So," he says, "she's not for you."

A jab of pain in my chest, but I ignore it. "No," I tell him. "She's not for me."

Even though every cell in my body revolts at the thought.

"This will be difficult without you."

"You'll manage," I mutter, hopping off the fucker, then moving to grab the gun I won't leave unattended, not even for a second—not with Matteo and his friends running around this yard on the regular.

I tuck it into the waistband of my pants, then turn and grab the fucker when he tries to run off, knocking him to the ground a second time.

He groans, holding his groin.

Felix sighs. "*Very* difficult."

"New Hampshire," I remind him as I pin the phone between my ear and shoulder, hefting the motherfucker who dared tramp through Lauren's flowerbeds up to his feet, marching him out of the yard, through the shadows of the neighboring yards.

I stop outside the expensive sedan I know he drove here.

Because I don't recognize it. Because it's Felix's style.

I dig into his pocket, find his keys, and bleep the locks before shoving the fucker in the passenger's seat. "You'd better come and clean up your mess."

Another chuckle. "And you'd better remove the bugs from her house."

I bite back a growl, hit a pressure point, watch as Felix's underling goes unconscious.

"Stay the fuck out of my life, Felix," I snap, ending the call and tossing the phone into the man's lap.

I disassemble the gun, making sure it can't ever be fired again, then shove it in the glove box so some idiot can't pick it up and try.

A scan of my surroundings as I slam the door, as I slip back into the shadows.

As I head back to Lauren's house.

Only this time, I head straight for the front door.

I KNOCK, and I don't do it quietly.

Then I wait, knowing that she's likely inside, trying to decide if she's going to answer the door.

She shouldn't—who the fuck knows who could be on her front porch.

I could call her. I have her number—not that she gave it to me, but because I can get anyone's number, anytime.

But that would require me giving her explanations I can't afford to give.

I bite that back, knock again, and I *still* don't do it quietly.

When I finish, I sense movement inside, can faintly hear footsteps on the floor coming close to the door, and I tense, trying to brace for what's going to happen next.

She peers through the window, and some part of me

settles because she took the time to take that look, didn't just whip the wooden panel wide and open herself up to whatever danger was lurking on her porch.

Her eyes widen when she takes me in there, and she stares at me for a moment before she seems to shake herself, brows slamming together as she disappears from sight.

I hear a *click* then the sound of metal sliding against metal, and then the door is pulled open.

"Pascal?" she asks, fucking beautiful without a lick of makeup, the flannel pajama pants and hoodie she must have pulled on after her bath doing nothing to show off the gorgeous curves I know are hidden below. "Is everything okay?"

I nod. "Can I come in?"

Teeth pressing into her bottom lip, and then she shakes her head, steps back. "Um, yeah. Sure."

I slip inside, looking around, taking in a view I've only seen from through the windows. She has a bulletin board with Matteo's drawings on the kitchen wall, a shoe rack loaded with rain boots and sneakers and flip flops, a row of hooks mounted into the sheetrock—and my jacket is there, hanging from one, as though it's waiting for me to walk through the door. I suck in a breath, focus on my surroundings instead of what the sight of my jacket suspended there makes me feel, and allow my gaze to keep moving. It slides toward a painting of the ocean filling up one wall in the blues and teals and purples I know that she prefers then around the rest of the space, trying to locate where Felix would have hidden the bugs.

Here near the door, for sure.

"Uhh," Lauren whispers. "Is there a reason that you showed up on my porch?"

A framed picture, near enough to the door to pick up on

any conversations, and because it's of her and Matteo, I know that Felix would see it as an extra fuck you to me.

"Can I get a glass of water?" I blurt.

Her brows furrow further, but to her credit, she just nods. "Yes, sure. Of course."

Then disappears into the kitchen.

I move quickly to the photo, run my fingers along the edges of the frame, and sure fucking enough, there's a goddamned bug there.

I yank it free, drop it to the floor, and crush it beneath the heel of my boot, managing to pocket the remnants just as she comes back in with my water.

"Sorry for the kids' cup," she murmurs, cheeks turning slightly pink. "I haven't had a chance to do dishes yet."

My eyes flick to the sink as I take a sip. "I'll help you."

"What—? No, Pascal, I—"

But I've already moved into the kitchen, using the chance to sweep my gaze around the room, searching for likely spots, identifying a handful even as I make a mental note to bring a team out to sweep the house tomorrow when Lauren and Matteo are at hockey practice, just to make sure I got them all.

"I'll wash," I say, setting my glass on the counter and moving to the sink. "You dry and put away."

"I have a dishwasher," she whispers. "I just...it's full and I was too tired to empty it."

I stop with my hands a couple of inches above the dishes and glance over my shoulder at her.

Beautiful, but with dark circles under her eyes. "You've got a lot going on," I say quietly, switching spots, shifting to the side and tugging open the dishwasher.

"You don't—"

I tug out a glass, hold it up. "Tell me where this goes, sweets."

Her nostrils flare and I'm barely able to keep my arm extended. Because—fuck—that shit just slipped out and I shouldn't have said it, God knows I *shouldn't* have said that. I promised myself that would never happen again. Not after—

Thankfully, she puts me out of the misery of my memories and tilts her head toward a cabinet to the left of the dishwasher. "They go there."

I nod, start unloading, taking advantage of Lauren doing the same to surreptitiously sweep the space for bugs.

It takes until I'm putting a mixing bowl away before I find it, tucked beneath the lip of granite on the underside of the island.

I pry it free, palm it, and then bring it to the sink, disabling it by running it under the hot water and crushing the components with the edge of a pot as Lauren finishes putting the silverware away. It goes into my pocket and then the rest of the dishes get washed.

"You know I was planning on getting these in the morning," she murmurs.

I look at her again, see those dark circles, know that she's constantly playing double duty, constantly having to be Mom and Dad. "I don't know Matteo all that well," I say as I rinse out a bowl, "but from what I *do* know, it doesn't seem like he ever runs out of energy."

Silence for long enough that I glance to the side, see that she's standing there, eyes soft.

When she catches me looking, she jerks, reaches for the glass I washed and sticks it in the top rack of the dishwasher. "No, he doesn't ever get tired," she says on a chagrined sigh, but when she meets my eyes, hers are dancing with humor. "But I don't want to miss a moment of it. I know he won't want me as much when he's older. Heck—" A wry twist of her mouth. "He's already abandoned me for his friends."

She looks like she needs a hug.

But I don't know how to do that, how to be the man to give her that and to not be *her* man in every sense of the word.

And...I'm not good for her.

Case in point? I'm searching her fucking house for bugs because my fucking past is...

Fucked.

And not just in regards to Felix, though I'm going to make sure that shit doesn't touch her.

Fucked in other ways that mean I *can't* touch her.

"So," I say, shoving that down and moving on from the pot, starting to scrub a plate, "it goes that dishes are less important than spending time with him."

Her breath hitches and she's quiet for a long moment. "Yes," she whispers. "That's true."

"And it goes to say that a woman who's got dark circles beneath her eyes and works her ass off for her kid can stand to cut herself some slack."

She inhales, exhales quietly. "You sound like Brit," she says quietly.

"Well," I tell her, my tone dry enough to bring a smile to her lips, "she had to learn it from somewhere."

EIGHT

Lauren

HE RINSES the last dish and passes it over to me, those dark brown eyes seeming to see right into my soul.

My heart skips a beat, and I look away, haphazardly stowing the dish in the bottom rack in a way that would have made Dave crazy.

But...he's dead.

I've had to learn to do things my way.

"Here."

I glance up, see Pascal holding a towel out for me to dry my hands.

Why does that make my heart flutter?

Probably because it's thoughtful, and paired with his words and the soft way he's staring at me...

Flutters. So many flutters I shouldn't be feeling.

"I—um—" I look away when his gaze locks onto mine. "You never told me why you're on my porch."

Clearly, nothing's wrong, considering he spent the last ten minutes washing dishes. And taking one sip out of the glass of water I got for him before rinsing it and passing it to me so I could put it in the dishwasher alongside the other stuff he cleaned.

"Didn't I?" he says, turning away and moving into the family room, his footsteps silent on the rug spread over the floor in the hall.

I follow him through the open doorway, across the entry-way, and into the room, arriving in the space just as he stops in front of the built-in shelves on either side of the fireplace and—

"Don't," I say without thinking as he starts to lift the frame I knocked over when he banged on my door and star-tled me.

He freezes, glances back at me.

"It's..." I nibble into my bottom lip, drift a little closer until I can see the flecks of gold in those dark eyes. "It's Dave," I whisper.

His big shoulders rise and fall on a breath, and then he shocks the shit out of me by lifting the picture frame, carefully setting it on the shelf. Only he doesn't tuck it to the side like I had. He puts it right in the middle of the center shelf and says, "You don't have to hide him. When we remember those we lost, we honor them."

I inhale sharply then find myself asking, "Who are you honoring?"

He goes still in that way of his—searching our surround-ings for a threat, for something that might hurt us.

But...the villain of this situation isn't tangible, isn't present in the room with us, forcing me to look down the barrel of a gun.

It's the past, the sickness, the...memories.

And I finally get that Pascal has them too.

Not memories—of course he has those. I'm not a freaking idiot. But...a past that is as sharp and as painful as mine.

Maybe...I study his face...

More.

My heart squeezes and I don't think, just lift my hand, pressing it lightly to his cheek.

He hisses out a breath and I start to pull back, but before my hand is a millimeter away from his skin, he's settled his on top of it, is pressing it more firmly against his face. "My wife," he whispers. "I lost my wife."

My knees wobble because the pain in my soul recognizes the pain in his.

"How?" I whisper.

"Home invasion," he says, and I jerk with surprise, partly because I can't believe quiet, secretive Pascal has actually told me. But also...

Because that doesn't happen.

Well, it does. It just—

Doesn't happen often.

And then something clicks in my mind.

"Is that why you got into security?"

A long pause, those pain-filled eyes on mine. "Yes," he says. "What I was doing...before"—he clears his throat—"meant I wasn't home to—" He stops, shadows clinging to, then covering, his suffering until he's quiet, secretive Pascal again, unfazed by everything. "I wasn't there." His tone hardens. "Now I am."

The last sounds like...a vow?

But before I can reply, he turns away. "Need to use the bathroom," he grinds out, walking from the room.

I stand there for a moment, staring into the open space, wondering if I should go after him, wondering if it's possible to come up with anything to say that doesn't come off as condescending or trite.

It's not your fault.

Clearly, he still has guilt and this man—this big, protective man with a huge heart and the past he's tried to bury—isn't going to shed it easily.

It doesn't matter if he wasn't there. It's the same red haze that coats my soul when I think of the persistent stomach pain Dave had, and how I didn't push for him to get it checked out.

Guilt and love, hurt and memories, they knot together really fucking tightly. They get so tangled, it's impossible to loosen the strands, to cling to the happy and put the hurt aside.

But as I touch the frame, I know that while I'm right, I also know that it's time—not to forget Dave, but to keep him close as I move forward.

Because I can't breathe under this blanket of the past.

And I need you to breathe, baby.

Dave's voice in my ears again.

It's less of a shock, less painful, and I swallow hard, blink away my tears, glance down at my naked ring finger.

Because...it's time.

"Yes," I whisper, pressing my fingertips to that photograph, to his face, committing his beautiful smile to memory. "I know."

Hold on.

Sew it deep.

But don't bury it.

Allow it to just...always be there, existing instead rising up in my throat and smothering me with sadness and making it so I can't remember the good times.

A smile and a happy day—that's what this picture was.

That's what I can remember.

I close my eyes, keep it close, and then I blow out a breath and turn away from the shelves, feeling the cold of the past receding as I walk across the rug, as I move toward what my life is going to look like. I know I'll be okay. I always am. But this is the first time those sentiments don't feel like a mantra I'm chanting and chanting until one day I hope it becomes true.

It feels...like reality.

And my future.

"Enough," I whisper, shaking that off and realizing that Pascal has been gone a long time.

I'm hoping he hasn't gotten lost...in my two-bedroom house.

Sure. That's totally likely.

Probably, he slipped back into the shadows and out of my life in that sneaky way he always manages to move, randomly showing up to fix things (and helping me acknowledge Dave and my past and that it's okay to move forward is definitely helping to fix things), and then disappearing like a puff of freaking smoke.

But he's not gone, I realize as I make it to the hallway and see him coming toward me.

"You okay?" I ask softly.

He smiles at me dismissively. "Yup. Fine." A nod toward the door. "I should—"

"Want to watch a movie?" I blurt.

He goes still, studies me closely for several moments.

"I mean," I say. "I'm not doing anything, and Matteo's at the sleepover, and there's that new action flick on streaming, and well, it's late and if you're hungry, I can make you—"

"No."

I blink, staring at him for a second before finding the

courage to ask, "No to the movie or me making you something?"

"The making."

"But"—it's hard to breathe past my heart beating rapidly in my chest—"not the movie?"

He nods, and I feel like I'm holding my breath until he says, "Yes, to the movie."

I exhale and it stutters when he adds, "I would like that very much."

It should be awkward, waiting while he toes off his shoes, sitting next to him on the couch, scrolling through the various apps until I find the movie and get it playing. But it's not.

If anything it feels...*normal*.

And maybe that's why I'm able to tuck my feet beneath me and relax.

Maybe that's why I don't flinch when he tugs the blanket off the back of the couch and drifts off.

Maybe that's why I don't protest when—much later—I'm barely nudged from sleep as I distantly feel him lifting me, cradling me close to his chest as he carries me down the hall.

Maybe that's why I fall right back to sleep when he tucks me into bed.

NINE

Pascal

I SHOULD HAVE GONE, but instead, I sat on the couch next to her and watched a completely unrealistic movie.

I should have gone, but instead, I stayed next to her as she dozed off, then tucked a blanket around her when she shivered in that peaceful sleep.

I should have gone, left her sleeping on her couch, warm in that blanket when the movie ended.

But as I stood up, intending to leave, my gaze was drawn back to her.

And I knew she would be uncomfortable in the morning, sleeping with her head propped up on one hand, her legs folded beneath her.

So...I did something incredibly stupid.

I scooped her up, carried her down the hall, and tucked her into bed.

And then I stood in the hall and I watched her settle back into sleep.

Watched as her body relaxed and her breathing steadied, lips parted, each exhale a soft puff.

Watched her as she dreamed and rolled to the side. Watched as—

"Pascal."

—she said my name.

That's when I realize insanity has taken over and do one more sweep of the house, looking for any remaining bugs, finding two more during my meticulous look. Which means I'll still be sending that team later today when she and Matteo are at hockey.

And now, I'm trying to find the strength to *keep* walking by the open door of the bedroom.

To walk *away* instead of sliding into bed next to her, holding her close, and—

The sun is coming up.

She's going to be awake soon.

And...I—

Can't stay.

So, I do what I do best.

I slip into the shadows, remain unseen as I get into my car...

And I go back to my empty office at the security center.

THE TEAM DOESN'T FIND any other bugs or cameras or any further signs of Felix's interference.

But I'm not an idiot.

I make arrangements so he knows I'm serious, and turn the screws so that the walls close in on him enough that he understands to not fuck with me.

To not fuck with Lauren or Matteo.

To not fuck with the Gold.

And I keep their house under surveillance.

Okay, fine, *I* surveil their house.

I'm there every fucking night for the next week, making sure that they're safe.

And every fucking night for that week, I have to resist going up their front door, have to resist knocking and pushing my way inside, have to force myself back into the shadows and to my car unseen and...

Back to my fucking office.

But at least tonight, when I stretch out on my couch, I finally get a text from Felix.

Jesus fuck, Manot. I said that I get you. Call off your fucking dogs.

I exhale, type out a message.

New. Hampshire.

A long pause. Then,

Understood.

And for the first time in one week, I breathe easily.

For the first time in weeks—or maybe, a lifetime—I *sleep* easily.

And I do it dreaming of Lauren.

I'M CLINGING to the shadows.

But...he finds me anyway.

"Do you want to come to dinner?"

I look up from the tiny human in front of me, and glance to where his mom is standing, apparently deep in conversation with Sara, Brit, and Mandy. But, as though she senses my stare, she looks up the moment my gaze hits her face, our eyes connecting.

Her brows flick up in question.

Or maybe, in challenge.

"Do you?" Matteo asks. "Everyone's coming back to our house because my mom is making lasagna and garlic bread and"—his nose wrinkles—"and we'll have to have salad too, but that's not the *worst* because we get to put dressing on it."

"On the salad?" I ask inanely.

A reluctant nod. "Yeah."

"I like salad," I tell him, getting my shit together. "It's brain food. The darker the leaves, the better."

He stops, considers that. "My mom says it's good for me."

"Your mom is right."

"I guess." He heaves a sigh. "So, do you want to come? My mom said you probably wouldn't."

Right. So, that flick of brows *had* been a challenge.

"Do you want me to come?" I ask.

Matteo nods before he says something that punches me right in the gut. "You're family. You should come to family dinner."

My throat...fuck, why is it tight?

"So, will you?" Matteo presses—and fuck, there goes my heart.

And...I can't do anything except nod.

He whoops softly, bumps the fist I lift, and then runs off to join the other kids sprinting around the indoor playground.

A location that's secure because we've hosted events here before, and because Delaney is at the door, managing who's coming and going. It's a location that I don't *need* to be inside of.

Except that some part of me couldn't stay away.

And now...I'm going to a family dinner, apparently.

Something that has equal parts of fear and...something

else flipping around my insides like goddamned monkeys playing on a high wire.

My gaze is drawn back to Lauren's, and I see her watching me. Our stares connect. Those brows lift again.

Challenge. Definitely challenge.

And...I bite back a curse.

Some part of me knows I'm not going to back down from it.

I start to knock then see the sign taped above the doorbell to *Come on in.*

It makes me want to turn around and run away.

But some force draws my hand to the knob and I turn it, push my way inside...

And find...chaos.

Kids are running around. Adults are laughing and drinking. The aforementioned lasagna smells fucking incredible. And I'm at a loss what to do.

Every light is on in the house, eliminating any shadows for me to hide in.

And as I move down the hall, my exit is quickly blocked by kids running through, and someone popping outside to grab a jacket, someone else taking the bag of trash to the can at the curb.

"You came!" Matteo says, skidding to a halt in front of me.

I nod.

He fist-pumps. "Awesome! Want to play soccer with us?" He hitches a thumb over his shoulder. "We're going out back."

"I should find your mom first," I say.

"Okay!"

And then he's off again, sprinting down the hall, and I

hear the clang of the back door opening and slamming shut. I turn for the kitchen—

"You came." A soft inquiry, but one that settles just as heavily on my heart.

"Yeah."

"Hmm." She folds her arms across her chest, leans back against the wall. "I was starting to think you were avoiding me."

I just look at her.

"Okay," she says after a moment. "I *know* you've been avoiding me." Her expression softens and she leans in, whispers, "I won't tell anyone about our conversation. I promise."

So fucking sweet that she thinks it's about me telling her something I shouldn't have.

So fucking sweet that she would keep my secrets.

So fucking sweet—

It has the words bursting out of me.

"I *was* avoiding you."

She exhales, something gentling in her demeanor, before she leans even closer. "Why?"

I clench my jaw then force myself to release it. "Because I don't know how to do this."

Because I'm not sure I *can* do this.

She reaches forward, takes my hand, and squeezes lightly. "We do it together," she whispers. "And by taking just one step at a time."

My stomach revolts at the very thought.

But...my heart does something else.

It rolls over, exposes its vulnerable underbelly, pulsing with...hope.

"So, what's the first step?" I find myself asking.

"Soccer," she says, mouth twitching.

TEN

Lauren

HE COMES in with a gleam of sweat on his forehead and a ravenous appetite.

But I've made enough lasagna and garlic bread to feed an army. (And enough Caesar salad to feed a slightly smaller one).

I dish up a bevy of plates for the soccer crew, lay them out on the island, and tell them to come and get it.

But because I know Pascal isn't going to take a plate from someone he might think would need it, that he'll stand back and wait for everyone to eat, even if that means he ends up with cold scraps (because that's all he thinks he deserves), I make him a special plate and bring it over to him.

Which also has the benefit of bringing me closer to him.

Because...moving forward.

Taking one step at a time.

And...maybe I want to take those steps forward with him.

There. I admitted it and didn't get struck down by lightning or burst into flames or become riddled with crippling guilt.

"Eat up," I say softly, pushing the plate into his hands.

He looks at me, those golden sparks in his eyes turning warm before he glances back down at his plate. "Salad?" he asks, glancing back up, those sparks now dancing with humor.

"It's good for you," I say softly.

"It's brain food!" Matteo chimes in, mouth full of romaine.

I lift my brows at Pascal, but his lips just twitch and he snags a plastic fork from the container I have perched in the middle of the island, scoops up his own forkful of salad and says, "Kid's not wrong." Then he shoves it into his mouth and grins over at Matteo.

They share a look that has my heart squeezing, and then they're eating and Matteo's talking—or really, rattling off a stream of information about his hockey team and his coach, about the Gold and the fact that Lucas sometimes shows up to help with practice, and then he's talking about his teacher and the sleepover he had the best time of his life at (his words) and then about his favorite YouTuber.

And the entire time, Pascal doesn't look impatient and isn't trying to extract himself from the conversation.

He's listening and engaged.

He asks questions, internalizes the answer, and...

My son is glowing.

Freaking *glowing*.

Which is why I know that this is right, these steps forward taken with a quiet, reserved man who relegates himself to the shadows.

It's why I know he needs help to see that he doesn't have to stay there.

And why I know I can be that person for him.

"You sure I can't stay and help?" Brit asks as Roxie pulls on her hand, nearly wrenching her bad shoulder out of its socket.

"No," I tell her with a laugh. "You've got your hands full." I nod toward Roxie, who's done another tug, making Brit wince. "You'd better go before Mandy has your head for messing up your shoulder."

Brit taps her nose. "Good point," she says. "I knew I kept you around for a reason."

She allows Roxie to finish pulling her out the door (and dragging her down the driveway toward her car), calling her goodbye as she folds her leanly muscled body into the driver's seat and pulls away from the curb.

And then there are no cars left.

Because Pascal's is...in whatever shadow he parked it in.

Sighing, I turn back for the house, pad inside, and lock the door behind me. I hear the soft drone of the TV and start for the family room, intending to tell Matteo to wrap it up and head to bed, but when I step onto the carpet, I see Pascal has my sleeping son in his arms. "I'll just tuck him into bed," he says softly.

"Yeah," I whisper, heart squeezing. "Thank you."

A nod, and then he starts moving forward, slowly and carefully, as though he's carrying the most precious cargo on the planet.

And he is.

My baby. My heart. My soul.

I exhale, shaking my head, pushing down the seriousness of my thoughts in lieu of...enjoying this moment.

This man who treats my son so kindly.

And who looks at me—

Like *that*.

My heart skips a beat as he strides back into the room

He slows to a stop and my breath hitches...because those sparks are—

Burning.

For me.

He clears his throat and looks away. "I'll get the dishes in the kitchen and—"

I move across the room, sneaky like a man who walks in the shadows.

And then I'm...toe-to-toe with him.

He doesn't move. Not one limb or finger or muscle. Not one inch.

Hell, I'm not even sure that he's breathing.

"Pascal?" I ask softly.

"Yeah," he rasps.

"Kiss me."

It's the bravest thing I've ever said, born of longing and need, loneliness and the way this man makes me feel.

But he still doesn't move—for long enough that my courage begins to erode and I find myself inching backward, putting some space between us—

Only I don't get there.

Because suddenly an arm is around my middle and a big, warm body is flush with mine and—

His mouth is descending.

His lips are hitting mine, tongue sweeping forward. I part and let him in, the kiss going from tentative and uncertain to intense enough to turn me to ash in the next heartbeat. I sigh in pleasure, melting against him, feeling all of those muscles, the hard planes of his body against the soft of mine, smelling him—man and spice and *mine*.

He groans as he yanks me closer, and then my feet are no longer on the floor. I'm in the air, his free hand encouraging me to wrap my legs around his waist, feeling—*oh my*—the hard length of his cock pressing against me as he turns, carries me to the couch, sinking down on it and—

Oh.

That's nice.

His big body pinning me to the cushions, the heavy weight of him sinking into me, making me feel—

Everything.

For the first time in forever, I feel *everything*.

I settle my hand over the back of his neck, keeping him close, never wanting to lose this feeling. I'm desperate to dive in, to allow it to surround me and suck me under and—

"Pascal," I moan as he releases my lips, dragging them over my jaw, back toward my ear, tongue ghosting over my earlobe, tracing the shell of my ear. "Oh God," I whisper.

Because it feels good.

It feels great.

It feels so fucking great that I lose any semblance of control.

ELEVEN

Pascal

ONE SECOND, I'm kissing her throat, intending to return to her mouth.

The next, I'm flat on my back with Lauren's lush body on top of mine, her legs straddling my middle, her breasts pushing into my chest. "God," she whispers, "You taste so good."

She presses her lips to my throat, to the underside of my jaw, and then to mine...and her kiss is—

Holy Fucking Hell.

Scorching. Fucking. *Hot.*

But it's going too fast.

We have to slow down.

This is too much and she might get hurt and—

Her tongue strokes along mine, her breasts press closer, and then I'm not thinking about slowing down, not thinking about anything except for her body beneath my hands, her soft moans in my throat, her pelvis rocking against mine.

She lurches back, breaking the kiss, reaching for the hem of her shirt, and ripping it over her head, tossing it to the side.

Fuck, she's pretty.

Breasts peeking out from behind cotton and lace, nipples beading beneath the fabric.

I want to peel that material free of her, want to get my mouth on her skin, want to taste and lick and suck every inch of her gorgeous body, and I lean in to do exactly that when my conscience yanks me hard, shaking me viciously until I focus.

Until I realize this is a big step from sitting next to her on the couch or eating dinner to...

Fucking.

I want to fuck her senseless.

And that's what finally helps me corral my desire. I roll us when she bends back down, pinning her to the cushions again, knowing this isn't helping my control—feeling her fucking gorgeous body beneath mine, knowing it would be so easy to rear back, to tug off her pants, to thrust inside—but needing to see her face, needing her to understand that I want her, but—

"Sweets," I murmur, unable to stop myself from dragging my lips along her throat. "We need to slow down."

She shudders, a soft sigh escaping her. "No, Pascal," she says. "We've both spent the last years in a stasis, trapped in a sticky amber while the rest of our world keeps moving forward." Her palm covers my cheek. "It's time we break free, and I want to do that with you."

My heart rolls over in my chest, and I look down at the beautiful woman splayed beneath me, her expression soft and warm and—

Fuck.

I want that too.

But...

I exhale.

She needs to know.

"I watched you," I admit. "At the practice rink. At the Gold games and team events. And...from the shadows of your yard."

Her brows drag together.

"At first, I couldn't believe how beautiful you were, even with the sadness in your eyes. And then I loved the way you interacted with Matteo and the other kids. I hated how close you grew to Lucas"—she grins—"And I was happy to see that you seemed to be settling in with the team."

Her fingers flex on my jaw. "But you didn't allow yourself the same."

"It's easier to live on the sidelines," I whisper. "No risk and I can disappear when it gets to be too much."

Her eyes slide closed then open. "You disappeared only to show up and watch me through my windows."

"I'm an asshole," I mutter. "I know I am."

"Why?" she asks, brows dragging together.

"Why did I watch you?"

A nod.

"Because I convinced myself you needed looking after." She scowls, and I gently peel her hand free, kiss her palm. "It was an excuse, sweets. I don't think I've ever met a woman as capable as you—"

"Except that last time you were over, I spent the night crying and had a sink full of dishes."

I smile, lean in and brush my lips over hers. "After you got up early to exercise and made your son breakfast before driving him to school. After you worked all day, including taking your last meeting in the car so you could pick him up and drive him to hockey practice—where you got him dressed, tied his skates perfectly, and saw him onto the ice then took another call, answered emails, and still managed to watch him score two goals in the scrimmage. Then you drove him to The Dairy for the team get-together, a place I know can't be easy for you to visit because before the shooting you used to walk through the winding paths surrounding it or sit on the grass for a few minutes during your lunch break, and now you don't go, unless it's for Matteo." I nuzzle at her jaw, say softly, "And then after all of that, you acquiesced to a sleepover that he wanted but made your heart hurt, came home and packed him a bag with anything he might need, and then you worried—through your dinner and your show and your bath but you still didn't turn me away when I randomly started pounding on your front door and barged my way inside. So," I tell her, straightening enough to run my lips over hers again, "I think you have capable down, baby."

"Those are the most words I've ever heard you say at one time," she whispers.

I run a hand over her hair. "Yeah, probably." I rest my forehead against hers, needing to focus on the important things, like—

"So, you'll cut yourself some slack?"

A breath. Then a nod. "Yeah." A beat, her eyes narrowing as they hold mine. "And you'll stop lurking in the shadows and just...come knock on my door?"

My heart pulses and fear rises up.

But she's right.

I want to be here, *right* here, and I've been inching toward it for months now, ever since I first saw her at the rink and wanted to do everything I could to eliminate the sadness from her eyes.

Which is why it's almost easy to say, "Yeah, sweets, I'll skip the shadows and knock on your door."

Her face brightens, and, fuck, I feel that deep.

She touches my jaw. "Good," she murmurs, and we stay still for a moment, our bodies pressed together, our gazes locked, silence between us. Until she says, "But you still never told me why you finally decided to stop watching me through my windows and instead came to my front door."

I know I have a choice here—hide it all and risk her being unprepared if it ever comes out, hurt that I hid things from her, upset that half of my life wasn't up for discussion, or...give her that part of me.

Slip from the hardening amber...

And live.

So, I tell her about Felix discovering my nighttime activities in her yard and the note, the man outside her house and the bugs inside. I tell her about what happened in New Hampshire and how that and what happened back at home, with losing my wife, my Mal, in such a violent way, I knew I needed to do something different. So I got out.

I give it all to her, my past and my heart offered up on a silver platter, and I make it clear that if this is too much, I will walk right back out to the shadows and leave her to build a beautiful life.

Wide eyes when I finally finish, her palm resting on my cheek. "Are we..." A breath. "Are we in danger?"

"No," I reassure her quickly. "I took care of it, made it very clear that I wouldn't ever work with him again."

Worry in the lines of her face. "How can you be sure?"

I touch her cheek. "Blackmail."

Shock slicing through expression. "Wh-what?"

"He's my ex-partner," I remind her. "And because of that, we did plenty of jobs together. He liked to run free and loose with laws and procedure—like with what happened on the job in New Hampshire I told you about"—she nods—"and I kept evidence of what he did. I have lots of it, including some things that could destroy his business. And if there's one thing that Felix cares about, it's his business." I cover her hand with my own. "So, I reached out to a few mutual contacts, turned a few screws, pushed a few buttons, and made it very clear that if he ever fucked around with you or Matteo or any of the Gold, he wouldn't have a job."

A nod, her fingers flexing. "And what about you?"

I frown. "What *about* me?"

"Did you make it clear he would face consequences if he messed around with you too?"

My heart squeezes. "I can take care of myself, sweets."

A long pause, those eyes seeing right into the depths of my soul. "Or you can let Matteo and I help with that."

Another squeeze in my heart. "Lauren."

She pulls my head down until my forehead rests against hers. "*Promise me* you'll let us look after you too—and it won't involve me looking through my windows, searching the shadows for a way to do it. Promise me it'll be inside this house over lasagna and salad and action movies," she whispers, pressing her hand to my chest, just over my heart. "Promise me you'll give us that."

I inhale, exhale. Then I push through the terror and cover her hand with my own. "I promise."

Her body relaxes, softens, melds with mine, and I know this is a step forward, one of many it will take to build something that will last a lifetime.

But it *is* a step.

No secrets. No hiding from the past. No shadows.

Just...sunshine.

I revel in that sunshine as she seals her lips over mine again, as her body starts undulating beneath mine, as her hands start working, dipping beneath the fabric of my tee, sliding over my skin, nails lightly raking. I shudder and rear back, lifting her in my arms and carrying her to the bedroom, stopping only to lock the door before I settle her on the mattress. Then I'm kissing her back, dragging my mouth over her body, stopping and paying homage to her breasts, her belly, her waist, and gorgeous hips. I flick open the button on her jeans, tugging the material down her legs, and—

Fucking beautiful.

I toss her jeans to the side, peel down her underwear, sending that to the floor too.

Then my mouth is on her, my tongue dragging through her labia, soaking up the sweetly tart evidence of her desire, circling her clit, and it's not long before I'm sucking and she's gasping, hands coming to my head, weaving into my hair, holding me to her as I drive her toward release.

Up, up, up and—

She pulls my head away from her.

"Together," she murmurs.

My heart—*fuck*—it's hers.

A bare moment later, I'm naked and pushing inside her, both of our soft groans mingling as our bodies move together, perfectly in sync, seeking that future.

Close now.

And then upon us, exploding and taking us under.

I cradle her close, listen to her breathing even out, soak in the feel of her against me and the brightness of this room, even though not a single light is on.

Because I know we're working toward another future.

TWELVE

Lauren

IT'S AN UNNATURALLY warm fall day, and since Matteo had the day off for a teacher work day and Pascal is running security for an event with the Rush hockey team (the Gold's AHL affiliate), we are playing hooky.

Or I am, anyway.

Calling in sick to work.

Taking the pulse on my kiddo.

Because it's been three months since that night at my house...and this weekend, Pascal is moving in.

So, I need to make sure that things aren't moving too fast for Matteo.

He seems to have taken the change in stride—hell, he's taken it in glee, especially because Pascal has been all in, at every sporting event and dinner, picking him up from school when I get stuck at work, taking us to his office and winning ultimate cool points by showing off all of the cutting edge tech he uses to keep his clients safe.

But because it's been so *all in*, the Mom in me needs to check in with my son.

Hence, the beach—sun and surf and boogie boarding in the cold as hell Pacific ocean, eating PB&Js tinged with sand, no matter that I wrapped them carefully in foil, and then following them up with individual bags of chips (Fritos for me, Doritos for him). Wresting cold, wet clothes off our bodies and dry ones on in the tiny beach-facing bathroom before stopping at the shop near the parking lot for popsicles—even though we're still freezing—and honey sticks, despite all of the sugar we've consumed.

And through all of that, I hear, "Maybe next time Pascal can come," a dozen times.

And I know...my son is okay.

Doesn't mean I won't keep checking in, but the worry in my heart about the next big step we're all taking this weekend settles.

The only bad part?

My cell took a dip in the Pacific.

Pockets, man, they're dangerous, especially when I forget to empty them and decide to leave my shorts on while showing off my elite boogie boarding skills.

It won't turn on, but I did my best to dry it, and hope that my tech-savvy boyfriend might have some tricks when I get home.

In the meantime, I tuck an extra towel around Matteo and do it smiling because his lids are already droopy.

He'll be out before I hit the highway.

That's okay.

We don't have any big plans for the weekend.

Nothing except building our future, one piece at a time.

Snoring hits my ears before I reach the 101 and continues for the rest of the drive, and I'm contemplating if I should circle the block a few times to give Matteo some extra time to sleep when I see commotion on my street.

One, two...*four* police cars with their lights flashing and a half-dozen nondescript others are parked...

In front of my house.

I gasp. "What the—?" I pull up to the curb and leave the engine running as I pop the door and get out.

Only to be stopped by a police officer. "Hang on, ma'am," he says. "This is a crime scene and you can't go—"

"That's my house," I tell him. "I need—" But my gaze goes beyond his shoulder and I see—

"Pascal!" I call, seeing him come out of my front door, walking and talking with the woman from The Dairy.

Delaney. Right.

They both turn in my direction, and I freeze.

Because *he's* frozen.

As though he cannot believe that I'm standing here.

Then he's running toward me, taking my arm, drawing me away from the officer and hugging me so tightly that I can barely breathe.

"What is it?" I rasp out. "What happened?"

He just keeps hugging me, and doing it for so long that my lungs protest.

"Pascal, honey, what happened?"

His arms tighten for a second before he releases me and steps back. "Someone busted your door open, burglarized your place."

I gasp, eyes tearing up.

My house. My pictures. Matteo's things.

"Oh my God," I whisper. "Is it...bad?"

"No," he whispers. "The TV in the front room is gone and the video game console. Some other electronics."

That wasn't great.

But it also...wasn't the worst.

"Pascal?"

Delaney comes up to us, stopping a couple feet away, gaze bouncing between us. "Cops picked up two teenagers the next block over. Van was loaded with stuff from Lauren's and what looks to be a handful of houses in the neighborhood. They're being taken downtown now."

Pascal nods.

Delaney walks away.

"You didn't pick up your phone," he rasps, gaze on his feet. "You didn't pick up your *fucking* phone."

"I accidentally dropped it in the ocean."

His head jerks, gaze hitting mine for a second, I think that might get through to him, shatter whatever ice has surrounded his mind and heart and soul so I keep pressing. "Baby," I say, reaching for him. "I'm okay. Matteo and I are both okay. I get that this must have—"

"Don't," he whispers, taking a step away from me.

"I—" My eyes flick toward my car. "Take a breath. Let's talk this through and—"

He shakes his head and backs up another pace. "I can't do this."

A hand plunges into my chest, grips my heart. "What are you saying?"

He shakes his head again.

I force my voice to remain calm. "I know this is triggering and that things are moving fast between us. If you want to pause for a second and talk through this. Maybe slow down and wait to move in—"

"No," he bursts out, the tone so harsh that fear slices through me. "I can't do this. I can't fucking do this."

"Pascal—"

"Ms. Hollows?" I jerk my head to the side, see the policeman I'd been talking to standing a couple of feet away. "Can we have a minute of your time?"

I glance at Pascal—see nothing but ice. "I know it's scary," I whisper. "But, please, just take *one* small step forward with me."

He closes his eyes, looks away.

"Ms. Hollows?"

I turn back to the officer. "Just a second. I'll be right over."

The officer nods, heads back to his squad car.

I rotate back to Pascal...

Only, he's gone.

Back into the shadows.

And I'm worried he's intending to stay there permanently.

THIRTEEN

Pascal

"YOU FUCKED UP," Delaney says, her body six inches from mine, "but you can still fix it."

"I already have," I mutter, turning away from her, eyes on the rows of empty desks in the security complex.

"So all of that crap you fed me about stepping out of the shadows was bullshit?"

I freeze, shoving down the fucking guilt, and turn back, snapping out, "An explanation of my life and my decisions is above your pay grade."

She rocks back, inhales sharply, but I don't let the hurt skating across her expression soften my resolution.

"You have a detail," I tell her. "Get on it."

Delaney looks at me, her eyes heavy with disappointment, and then she shakes her head and walks away, saying, "So fucking typical."

Fucking *finally*.

I walk past the empty desks, shove into my office, and set about working myself into exhaustion, working until I get so fucking tired I can't safely drive over to Lauren's place and keep doing shit I shouldn't have started in the first place.

It's only, hours later that I know I'll be able to slip into peaceful oblivion—at least for a little while.

Because I have no doubt that my dreams will be filled with Lauren's gentle eyes and Matteo's crooked smile...

"Fuck," I hiss, rubbing a hand over my head, trying to remind myself why I'm here, why I think I can't do this, why I didn't stay and hug Lauren and Matteo tightly, acknowledging that this shit scared me, and did it deep, and—

I can't.

It wells up in me again, and I lock my computer, shove back from my desk, stride over to my couch.

Not tired now.

But I'm going to force myself to sleep anyway, even if it's riddled with Lauren and Matteo, even if it doesn't come— likely—and I end up wide awake, staring at the ceiling, thinking about them all fucking night—

"Enough," I growl, flopping onto the couch and then immediately jumping back up to my feet when something jabs me in the back. "Christ," I mutter, reaching down, seeing the action figure—

And knowing that I seriously—*seriously*—fucked up.

One step at a time.

One *fucking* step.

And instead, I'd spun around, leaped backward and...

I fucked up.

"Shit," I mutter, turning for my desk, intending to grab my keys, my phone, and drive back to Lauren's place and pound on the door, no matter that it's fucking late.

But just as my fingers grip my keys, the exterior perimeter sensor goes off.

"What the fuck?"

I jab at my keyboard, pull up the cameras, and see—

Lauren is attempting to breach the exterior door, jabbing at the keypad, yanking at the handle, knocking on the door.

I hit a button to turn on the speakers—

"You'd better open this damned door, Pascal!" she shouts. "Right fucking now. You don't get to walk back out of our lives and hide in the darkness just because you got scared!" She bangs again and I swear to fuck that I can actually hear it reverberating through the warehouse. "You—you—*coward!*"

The word is like acid to my ears, but it's not like I don't deserve it.

Running scared.

Running away.

Back into the shadows of my life.

Pound. Pound. Pound.

"You had better let me in and—"

I hit the button to buzz open the door.

She freezes, and I watch her for just a moment longer on the cameras. She takes a breath and holds it for a second. Then she pulls open the door and disappears from view.

I'm already moving, pushing out of my office, walking by the rows and rows of empty desks.

Out into the hallway.

Through the door into the garage.

And...she's there.

Right *there.*

Her angry steps halt and she skids to a stop.

Then her chin comes up and she crosses her arms, glaring at me. "I can't believe—"

I go to her, plunging one hand into her ponytail, knocking the tie loose, the other dropping to her waist, yanking her flush against me. "I'm sorry," I say before dropping my head and kissing her with every bit of what I feel for her.

And it's a fucking lot.

It's *everything*.

"I love you," I say, breaking away.

"Wh-what?" she sputters.

I cup her cheek. "I love you and I panicked and I'm sorry." I kiss her again. Break away again. "And it won't happen again, sweets. Not ever. I promise."

Her eyes are wide and her lips are swollen.

And her body has melted against mine.

But she's capable, as always, because she reaches up and cups my jaw, tilting my face down toward hers. "Thank you for apologizing," she whispers.

"I—"

A finger over my lips.

"I wasn't done," she says firmly.

I kiss the tip of it. "Okay, baby," I murmur. "Go on."

A pert look. "Thank you for apologizing."

I nod, but don't interrupt this time.

"But," she says, sliding that hand to my jaw, cupping it lightly, locking our gazes together. "I don't want you to be hard on yourself."

My brows lift, and it's much harder to not interrupt now.

"We're just starting," she says. "We're going to mess up. We're going to make mistakes and get mad or scared or need space." She drops her hand. "And that's okay."

"It's—"

She presses that finger to my mouth a second time.

"It's *okay* because"—she smiles—"You can run, baby. But you can't hide. Not from me. Not from what I feel for you. Not from *our* love."

"Fuck," I whisper.

Her hand drops to my chest, resting over my heart, probably feeling that it's pounding beneath my rib cage.

"I love you," I tell her.

She smiles. "I love you too."

Fuck, that feels...like *every-fucking-thing*.

And I have to draw her close, have to kiss her again.

She drops back onto her heels. "You're moving in."

Not a question. An order.

And one I don't mind acquiescing to.

"I'm moving in," I whisper, taking her hand. "Now." I freeze as something occurs to me. "Where's Matteo?"

"At Brit's."

Of course she wouldn't leave him alone.

"We'll pick him up on the way home," I say, giving an order of my own.

Warmth in her eyes, in the way she holds tightly to my hand. "Sounds good, baby." She tilts her chin toward the hallway. "After we get your stuff."

"Right." I draw her back through the halls and into my office then pick up my bag from where it's shoved into the corner.

"That's all?" she asks as I snag my keys, shove my phone into my pocket, and start drawing her back out.

I shrug. "I travel light."

She squeezes my hand. "Well, we're going to change that."

I can see it now—a house full of kids, a garage overflowing with boxes, a minivan packed with suitcases and backpacks, a cooler and all manner of kid gear.

Extracurriculars and homework. Getting up at dawn on Saturday for a soccer game.

Sleepless nights and broken bones and animated movies constantly on TV.

It should be a nightmare.

But instead...it's beautiful, golden sunlight.

Hate missing Elise's new releases? Love contests, exclusive excerpts and giveaways?

Then signup for Elise's newsletter here!

www.elisefaber.com/newsletter

And join Elise's fan group, the Fabinators (https://www.facebook.com/groups/fabinators) for insider information, sneak peaks at new releases, and fun freebies! Hope to see you there!

I so appreciate your help in spreading the word about my books, including sharing with friends! Please leave a review on your favorite book site!

GOLD HOCKEY SERIES

Gold Hockey (all stand alone)
Blocked
Backhand
Boarding
Benched
Breakaway
Breakout
Checked
Coasting
Centered
Charging
Caged
Crashed
A Gold Christmas
Cycled
Caught
Cap
Covered
Crushed

Changed
Scored

Rush Hockey Trilogy #3

Puck and Make Up

Blinded By Pucks

Match Made in Pucks

Eagles Hockey Series (all stand alone)

Broken Laces

Knotted Laces

Lace 'em Up

Billionaire's Club (all stand alone)

Bad Night Stand

Bad Breakup

Bad Husband

Bad Hookup

Bad Divorce

Bad Fiancé

Bad Boyfriend

Bad Blind Date

Bad Wedding

Bad Engagement

Bad Bridesmaid

Bad Swipe

Bad Girlfriend

Bad Best Friend

Bad Rebound

Bad Romance

Bad Business

Bad Billionaire's Quickies

Love, Action, Camera (all stand alone)

Dotted Line

Action Shot

Close-Up

End Scene

Meet Cute

Love After Midnight (**all stand alone**)

Rum And Notes

Virgin Daiquiri

On The Rocks

Sex On The Seats

Life Sucks Series

Train Wreck

Hot Mess

Dumpster Fire

Clusterf*@k

FUBAR

Perfect Storm

Free Fall

Lost Cause

Roosevelt Ranch Series (**all stand alone, series complete**)

Disaster at Roosevelt Ranch

Heartbreak at Roosevelt Ranch

Collision at Roosevelt Ranch

Regret at Roosevelt Ranch

Desire at Roosevelt Ranch

Phoenix Series (**read in order**)

Phoenix Rising

Dark Phoenix

Phoenix Freed

Phoenix: LexTal Chronicles (**rereleasing soon, stand alone, Phoenix world**)

From Ashes

In Flames

To Smoke

KTS Series (all stand alone, series complete)

Riding The Edge

Crossing The Line

Leveling The Field

Scorching The Earth

Cocky Heroes World

Tattooed Troublemaker

ABOUT THE AUTHOR

USA Today bestselling author, Elise Faber, loves chocolate, Star Wars, Harry Potter, and hockey (the order depending on the day and how well her team -- the Sharks! -- are playing). She and her husband also play as much hockey as they can squeeze into their schedules, so much so that their typical date night is spent on the ice. Elise is the mom to two exuberant boys and lives in Northern California. Connect with her in her Facebook group, the Fabinators or find more information about her books at www.elisefaber.com.

facebook.com/elisefaberauthor

amazon.com/author/elisefaber

bookbub.com/profile/elise-faber

instagram.com/elisefaber

tiktok.com/@elisefaberauthor

goodreads.com/elisefaber